I Want to go Home, Alice McLerran, Tambourine Books, 32 pp. Ages 4 and up: One of the most traumatic events in a child's life occurs when he has to move. Two newly published books — one a picture book for young children, the other a book written for middle grade readers — address the effect of mov-ing on a child. In **I Want to go Home,** Marta doesn't like living in her new house, and neither does Sammy, the cat her mother gives her to try to cheer her up. He won't eat or drink the food put out for him, and hides from Marta in the shadowy corners of the new, strange house. In trying to comfort the frightened cat, Marta forgets her own loneliness. The next morning when Sammy finally jumps into Marta's lap and begins to purr, Marta says, "You see? Everything's going to be okay. This is home now." And she realizes it is.

Alice McLerran

I WANT TO
GO HOME

pictures by **Jill Kastner**

Tambourine Books / New York

Library of Congress Cataloging in Publication Data
McLerran, Alice   I want to go home/by Alice McLerran;
pictures by Jill Kastner.—1st ed. p.   cm.
Summary: A new cat named Sammy helps Marta
adjust to the move to a new house.
[1. Cats—Fiction.   2. Moving, Household—Fiction.]
I. Kastner, Jill, ill.   II. Title.
PZ7.M47872Iaw   1992 [E]—dc20 91-9599 CIP AC
ISBN 0-688-10144-5 (trade) — ISBN 0-688-10145-3 (lib.)
10 9 8 7 6 5 4 3 2 1
First edition

For Mandy and Mozart

A.M.

For Philip

J.K.

Marta glared at the walls of the new bedroom. "Purple and yellow flowers," she said. "YUCK."

Mama was moving Marta's clothes into the closet. "Some people like wallpaper."

Marta thought about her bedroom back home. Suddenly a horrible idea struck her. "Those new people—they wouldn't put yucky wallpaper in *my* bedroom, would they?"

"Let's hope not," Mama said.

"Well, even if they do, when we go home again we can paint it back," said Marta.

Mama hugged her. "This is home now, Marta."

"Not for me," said Marta. "I want to go *home*."

Mama kept talking about how Marta would make new friends soon, about how nice their new house was. But that night Marta huddled in bed trying hard to pretend she was back in her room at home.

The next day Mama carried in a funny-looking cardboard box. Marta peeked through one of the holes. Another eye was peeking out. "What's *that*?" she asked.

"That's Sammy," said Mama. "His old owners are moving into a place that doesn't allow pets. You've been wanting a cat, so—"

"Oh, that was when I was home," said Marta. "Here it doesn't matter." But she opened the top to get a good look.

There was Sammy, looking back at her. He leapt from the box, and stared at her once more. Marta reached for him, but he hissed and ran from the room.

"He doesn't want to live in this place, either," said Marta.

"We'll have to make sure he doesn't slip outside," said Mama.

Marta shrugged—but she helped Mama put cat food and water in a corner of the kitchen. They fixed a litter box out next to the washing machine.

And now where was Sammy?
Marta peered under all the beds,
under all the dressers and
nightstands.
Sammy?
She looked behind the shiny
new refrigerator and stove.
Sammy?
She checked under the familiar
sofa and chairs and behind all the
draperies.
Sammy?

She climbed up the attic stairs. Just rafters and space, and the smell of wood and dust—no place there for a cat to hide.

She went down to the basement and rummaged through all the open cartons, through dolls and dishes, books and blankets.

No Sammy.

He wasn't anywhere.

"He's gone," she told Mama. "He's gone back to his old home."

Mama shook her head. "Sammy can't have left the house. If we wait, he'll come out."

When Marta was ready to go to bed the cat food and water still hadn't been touched. Once more Marta searched, room by room. Was that . . . ? No, it must have been her own shadow.

Sammy?

No sign of a cat anywhere.

In bed, in the dark, she listened hard. The whole house was quiet. He has to be here, she told herself. Hiding somewhere alone, missing his old home.

In the morning all the cat food was still in the dish—not a bite eaten. "Are you *sure* Sammy is here?" asked Marta.

Mama nodded. "We just have to be patient."

But they didn't see him all that day. "Sammy must be getting awfully hungry," said Marta.

After she got into her nightgown that night, Marta tried to put her jeans on the closet shelf, the way she did at home. But this shelf was too high to reach. Stupid closet, she thought. She wadded her clothes into a ball and hurled them up there.

Something shot out.
Sammy!

The minute he landed he
streaked under Marta's bed.
Marta peered underneath it; he
was cowering close to the wall, out
of reach. Well, at least he's here,
thought Marta. But poor Sammy.
So sad and scared.

She closed the door to keep him
with her, climbed into bed, and
turned out the light. "Don't be
afraid," she told Sammy softly. "I
wasn't trying to hit you. We'll take
good care of you. Pretty soon
you'll be happy here."

There was no sound from under
the bed. Sammy still had to be
there, though. She kept trying to
comfort him until she couldn't stay
awake any longer.

The next day Sammy did come out to explore the house. He finally ate a little of the food and drank some of the water. But if Marta tried to touch him, he always ran right back under her bed. "Come on," said Marta, "we're nice people!"

Mama ruffled Marta's hair lightly and smiled. "It won't be long before Sammy feels more at home," she promised.

Late that night, Marta woke with a start. Something had just jumped up onto the foot of her bed. Sammy! She could feel his steps walking cautiously up the bed. They stopped near her shoulder. Would he stay? At last she felt him relax and settle next to her. Very, very slowly she reached one hand toward him. Very, very gently she started to pet him. Sammy didn't purr—but he didn't run away. Marta kept stroking him until they both fell asleep.

The next morning Sammy didn't try to hide. He just stayed on the bed, washing himself. When Marta went out to the kitchen for breakfast, so did Sammy. He walked right to his dish and started eating.

After breakfast Sammy followed Marta into the living room, and the minute she sat on the couch he jumped onto her lap. As she ran a finger gently under his chin, she could feel a purr starting. "You see?" said Marta. "Everything's going to be okay. This is home now."

Hey, she thought.

It *is*.